WHAT A BEAUTIFUL NAME

STORY BY

Brooke and Scott Ligertwood & Ben and Karalee Fielding

ILLUSTRATIONS BY

Scott Ligertwood

WHAT A BEAUTIFUL NAME

All Scripture quotations and paraphrases are taken from the Holy Bible, New International Version®, NIV®.
Copyright © 1973, 1978, 1984, 2011 by Biblica Inc.™ Used by permission of Zondervan. All rights reserved worldwide, www.zondervan.com.
The "NIV" and "New International Version" are trademarks registered in the United States Patent and Trademark Office by Biblica, Inc.™

Hardcover ISBN 978-0-593-19270-2 • eBook ISBN 978-0-593-19271-9

Copyright © 2020 by Ben Fielding, Karalee Fielding, Scott Ligertwood, and Brooke Ligertwood

Published in the United States by WaterBrook, an imprint of Random House, a division of Penguin Random House LLC.

WATERBROOK® and its deer colophon are registered trademarks of Penguin Random House LLC.

The Library of Congress catalog record is available at https://lccn.loc.gov/2019054908.

Printed in China

Cover design by Anna Bauer Carr; cover illustration by Scott Ligertwood

2020—First Edition

10 9 8 7 6 5 4 3 2 1

SPECIAL SALES

Most WaterBrook books are available at special quantity discounts when purchased in bulk by corporations, organizations, and special-interest groups. Custom imprinting or excerpting can also be done to fit special needs. For information, please email specialmarketscms@penguinrandomhouse.com.

FOR

Harper, Leopold, Ella, Dylan, and Rooney

On a regular Monday, in Oliver's room,
    in through the door came a familiar tune.
His mother was singing a sweet melody.
    "About who, though?" he wondered.

"What Name could it be?"

WHAT A BEAUTIFUL NAME IT I

He couldn't recall,
    but he knew
    that he knew,

there must be an answer; there must be a clue.

THIS CALLS FOR ADVENTURE!

He grabbed his friend Leo, his backpack and cap,

some snacks and some water, his tent and his map.

LEO

With imagination and teamwork, they planned for their trip.

STEP ONE:

Build a bright
yellow rocket ship!

Up!

Up!

Up!

up!

They flew over mountains, majestic and tall,
and as they went higher, they watched Earth grow small.
They counted the stars (or at least they tried!),
and Oliver wondered,

"WHO hung them here, so way up high?"

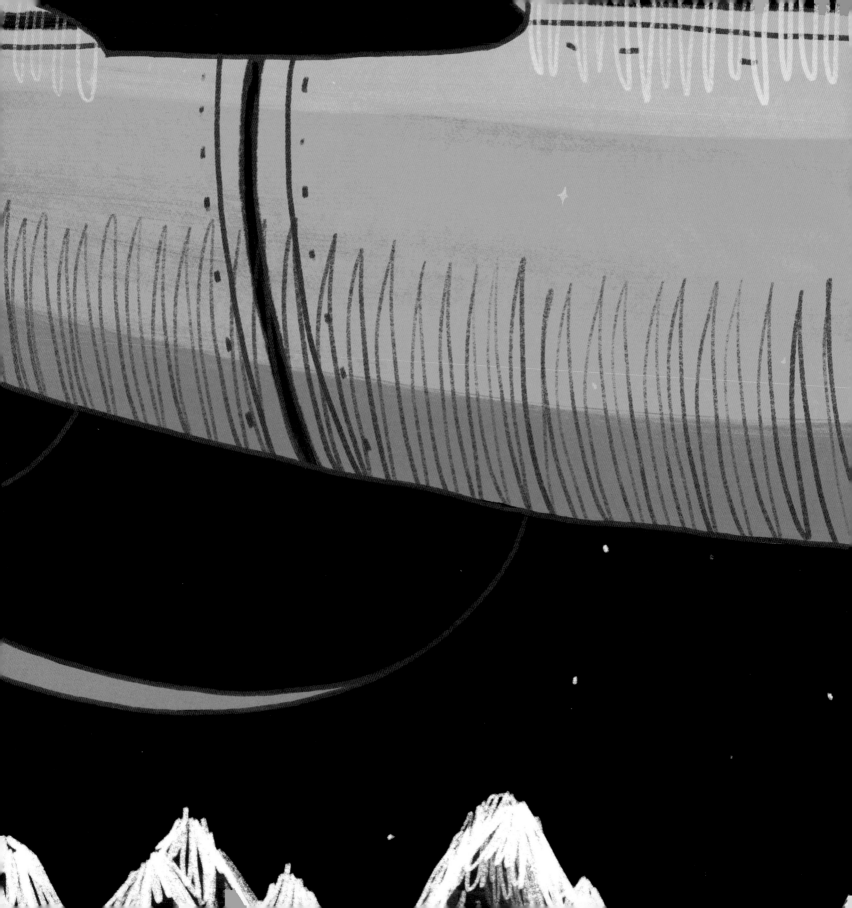

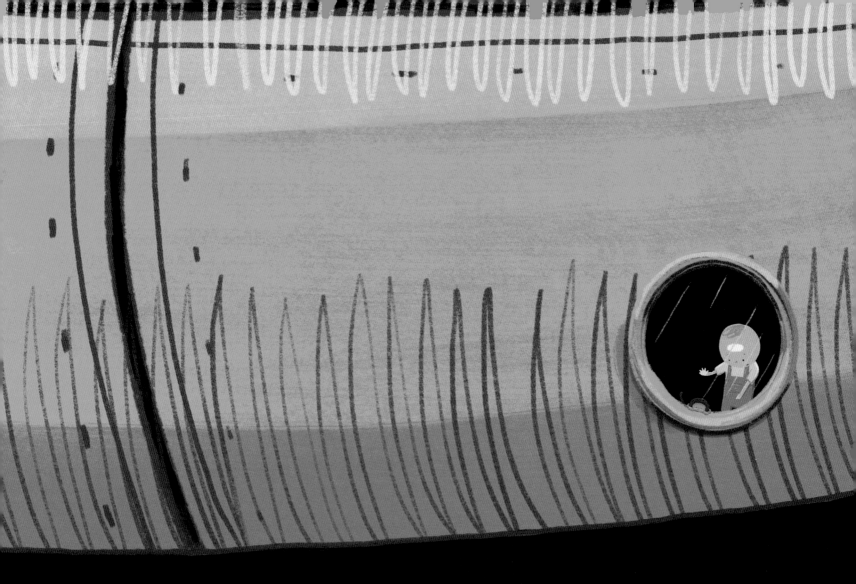

Then floating along in the great open skies,
with beauty now filling his heart through his eyes,
the words to the song drifted into his brain:

"Oh, this really must be a BEAUTIFUL Name!"

VVVRRRROOOOOOO

OOOOOOOOOOOOMM!!

They set up their tent
        and studied their map

and told funny stories
        and shared all their snacks.

They danced

and they sang

late into the night,

excited to set out again at first light.

HA HA HA!!!

Grateful for friendship and good company,
they continued their quest—this time on the sea!

The Name that they searched for felt closer and nearer,
and Oliver's longing to know it grew clearer.
With wide eyes, he looked all around and exclaimed,

"This really must be a **WONDERFUL** Name!"

Then the ocean grew darker and wilder and wider.
The waves rose like giants, higher and higher.
But his heart held on tight to the words that were true . . .

"The Name is not just BEAUTIFUL and WONDERFUL but POWERFUL too!"

Crossing the ocean,
        they landed on shore,

where wild things grow
        and the animals roar.

There in the shade of a palm, they would rest,
    recounting the clues they had found on their quest.
And lying there, thinking how far they had come,
    Oliver's mind wandered home (where their search had begun)

Then, remembering a moment in church,
Oliver jumped up all excited:

"I KNOW WHERE TO SEARCH!"

"One Sunday, we kids were singing this song . . .
What if the Name's in a book we've known all along?"

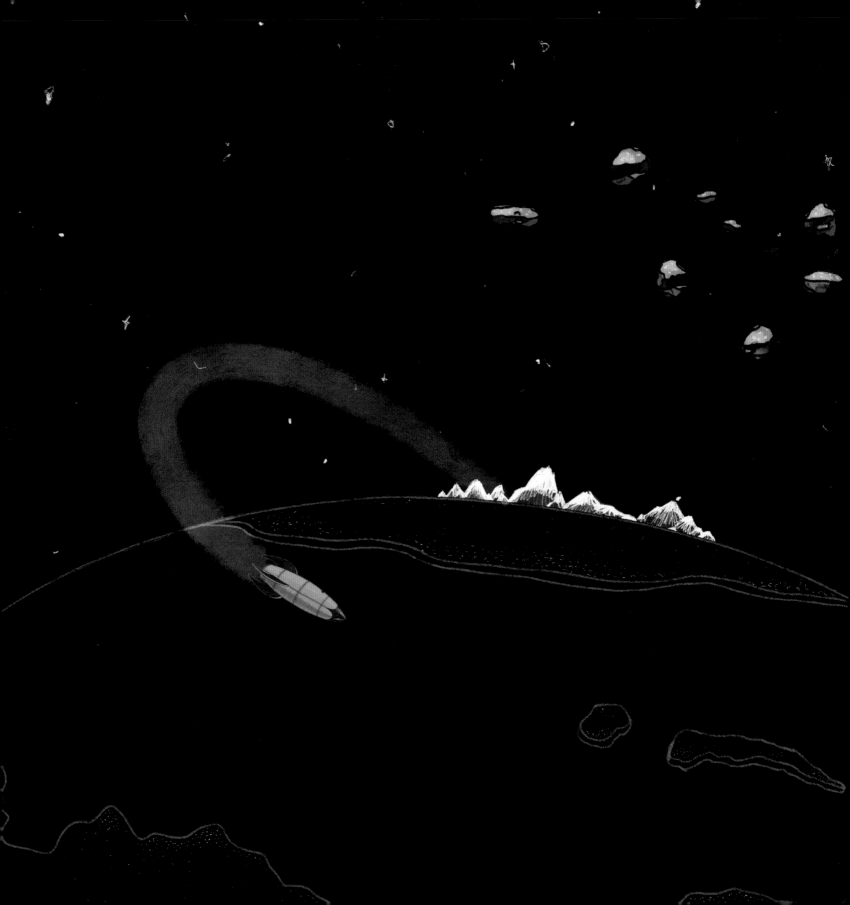

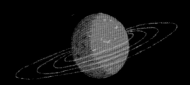

So out of the jungle and over the seas,
Leo and Oliver raced at full speed.

Then over the mountains to Oliver's door,
they dashed for the books that covered the floor.

"It's this one!" cried Oliver, holding the book.
And opening his Bible, he knew where to look . . .

CREATOR and SAVIOR,

who made everything,

BEAUTIFUL, WONDERFUL, POWERFUL KING!

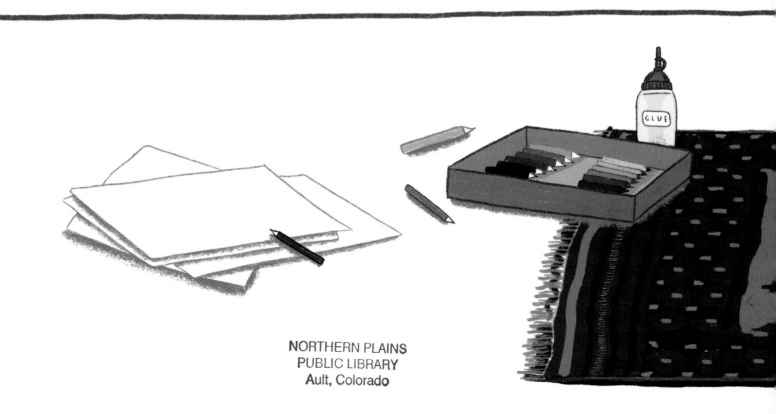

He'd known all of this before blasting off!
Before setting sail, before jungles and rocks!

In boats and in rockets and tents out in space,
the Name had been with them in every place.

And the most BEAUTIFUL, WONDERFUL, POWERFUL part?

It was the Name of the person alive in his HEART...

Their adventure had paused ('cause adventures don't end),
and Oliver, yawning, snuggled his friend.

Dozing to dreamland, he heard that same song,
about the Name of all names that he'd known all along . . .

WHAT A BEAUTIFUL NAME

Words and music by Brooke Ligertwood & Ben Fielding

VERSE 1

You were the Word at the beginning, one with God the Lord Most High
Your hidden glory in creation now revealed in You our Christ

CHORUS 1

What a beautiful Name it is, what a beautiful Name it is
The Name of Jesus Christ my King
What a beautiful Name it is, nothing compares to this
What a beautiful Name it is, the Name of Jesus

VERSE 2

You didn't want heaven without us, so Jesus You brought heaven down
My sin was great, Your love was greater
What could separate us now?

CHORUS 2

What a wonderful Name it is, what a wonderful Name it is
The Name of Jesus Christ my King
What a wonderful Name it is, the Name of Jesus
What a wonderful Name it is, the Name of Jesus

BRIDGE

Death could not hold You
The veil tore before You
You silence the boast of sin and grave
The heavens are roaring the praise of Your glory
For You are raised to life again
You have no rival, You have no equal
Now and forever God You reign
Yours is the kingdom, Yours is the glory
Yours is the Name above all names

CHORUS 3

What a powerful Name it is, what a powerful Name it is
The Name of Jesus Christ my King
What a powerful Name it is, nothing can stand against
What a powerful Name it is, the Name of Jesus

A LETTER TO PARENTS

Dear Grown-Up,

We are ardent believers that the worship songs we sing with our children should be firmly founded in Scripture. Our prayer is that poetry and song serve as invitations and access points to the power of God's truth, deepening our understanding and worship of an indescribable God.

The Bible can be complicated, even for adults. There are verses, chapters, and entire books that will take more years to grasp than we may have on earth. Understanding and exploring the Bible really is a lifelong pursuit. But here's the thing: we've sat and watched our little ones sing this song at the top of their lungs—and mean every word. The Bible and worship is just as much for our babies as it is for us. Jesus said it Himself: "Let the little children come to me, and do not hinder them, for the kingdom of heaven belongs to such as these" (Matthew 19:14). Rather than assume our kids can't understand these biblical truths, we assume that God is already speaking to them, and we've tried our best to encourage their understanding. So we wanted to take a moment to share some of the scriptural inspiration behind the song "What a Beautiful Name" so that your time together reading this book would be rich and add to the wisdom, stature, and favor that was declared over Jesus as He grew also (Luke 2:52).

THANK YOU for taking the time to read, teach, and celebrate these cherished truths with the little people in your life.

Our words and songs will never fully describe the glory, beauty, wonder, and power of our God; they will only ever be an imperfect attempt at describing a perfect God. As we worship, though, we move nearer to the God who has shown time and time again that He desires to be near us.

May your time together with the little people in your life be filled with laughter, memories, good conversation, adventure, and the wonder of worshipping a God whose Name is more Beautiful, Wonderful, and Powerful than we could ever describe.

You're doing a really good job.

With love,

Brooke and Scott, Ben and Karalee

VERSE 1

You were the Word at the beginning
One with God the Lord Most High
Your hidden glory in creation
Now revealed in You our Christ

Verse 1 begins with Jesus, the Word, at the beginning of all creation: He was with God and was (and is!) God (John 1:1). The mysteries of our infinitely beautiful and glorious God, one hidden for generations, have now been revealed through Jesus (Colossians 1:26). When Jesus took on flesh, we (humanity) got to see the glory of God (John 1:14); the Name of Jesus reveals the beauty and glory of God.

VERSE 2

You didn't want heaven without us
So Jesus You brought heaven down
My sin was great, Your love was greater
What could separate us now?

"Father, I want those you have given me to be with me where I am, and to see my glory, the glory you have given me because you loved me before the creation of the world" (John 17:24).

While God is all sufficient, all powerful, and all knowing, the God of creation and of eternity, He is also the God whose love surpasses knowledge (Ephesians 3:19). In verse 2, we wanted to describe the love of God, who, though in need of nothing, "so loved the world that he gave his one and only Son, that whoever believes in him shall not perish but have eternal life" with Him (John 3:16).

BRIDGE

Death could not hold You
The veil tore before You
You silence the boast of sin and grave
The heavens are roaring
The praise of Your glory
For You are raised to life again
You have no rival
You have no equal
Now and forever God You reign
Yours is the kingdom
Yours is the glory
Yours is the Name above all names

The death of Jesus tore the veil of the temple (Matthew 27:51) that, put simply, separated people from the presence of God. We now have access to God through the death of Jesus. But death could not hold Him, and sin and death have ultimately lost any power (Romans 6:9), for Jesus rose to life again. The heavens are roaring with the praises of His glory and power (Revelation 19:1). Although variations of the phrase "Yours is the kingdom, the power, and glory forever" cannot be found in Jesus's original prayer in Matthew 6 (the Lord's Prayer), the words have been used as a corporate conclusion to that prayer for centuries. We varied that phrase slightly by saving the word *power* for the final chorus and adding "Yours is the Name above all names" (Philippians 2:9) as a fitting summary of the beauty, wonder, and power that is in the Name of Jesus.

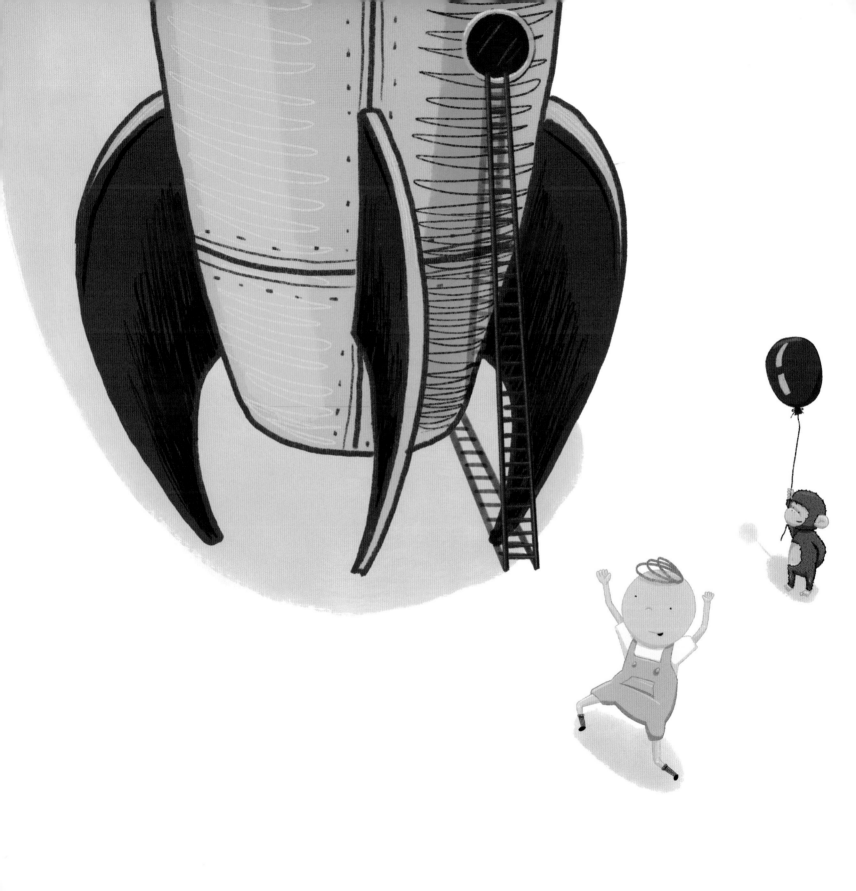